♡ Trip to the Pumpkin Farm ♡

Read more
OWL DIARIES
books!

OWL DIARIES

♡ Trip to the Pumpkin Farm ♡

Rebecca Elliott

SCHOLASTIC INC.

For the Peacock family,
my flap-tastic feathery friends who
are always up for a party. —R.E.

Library of Congress Cataloging-in-Publication Data

Names: Elliott, Rebecca, author. | Elliott, Rebecca. Owl diaries ; 11.
Title: Trip to the Pumpkin Farm / by Rebecca Elliott.
Description: First edition. | New York, NY : Branches/Scholastic Inc., 2019.
| Series: Owl diaries ; 11 | Summary: Eva Wingdale and her class are excited about their trip to Poppy's Pumpkin Farm, where every year, there is one very large, extra special, Thank-You Pumpkin; but on the second day of the visit the owls find that the Thank-You Pumpkin has gone missing, and the farm animals are in an uproar—so Eva and the other owls turn detective to solve the mystery of the missing pumpkin.
Identifiers: LCCN 2018053289 | ISBN 9781338298642 (pbk. : alk. paper) | ISBN 9781338298659 (hardcover : alk. paper)
Subjects: LCSH: Owls—Juvenile fiction. | Animals—Juvenile fiction. | Pumpkin—Juvenile fiction. | Sharing—Juvenile fiction. | Diaries—Juvenile fiction. | Detective and mystery stories. | CYAC: Mystery and detective stories. | Owls—Fiction. | Animals—Fiction. | Pumpkin—Fiction. | Sharing—Fiction. | Diaries—Fiction. | LCGFT: Detective and mystery fiction.

Classification: LCC PZ7.E45812 Tr 2019 | DDC [Fic]—dc23 LC record available at https://lccn.loc.gov/2018053289

10 9 8 7 6 5 4 3 2 1   19 20 21 22 23

Printed in China   62
First edition, August 2018

Edited by Katie Carella
Book design by Maria Mercado

♡ Table of Contents ♡

♡ That Fall Feeling! ♡

Sunday

Hi Diary,

It's me again, Eva Wingdale! Don't you just love autumn? The colors look **HOOTIFUL**! <u>And</u> there's a Treetopolis holiday coming up — Falling Leaves Day! It celebrates the first day of autumn. But more about that later . . .

<u>I love</u>:

School trips

Hugs

The word <u>cobweb</u>

<u>Pumpkin</u> Pie

(Don't you just love that
word, too!?)

Costume parties

Playing in
leaf piles

Finding lost
things

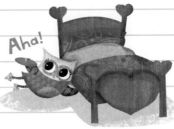

Aha!

Getting cozy
by the fire

I DO NOT love:

Trying to fall asleep when I'm excited about tomorrow

Tripping and falling

The word <u>worm</u>

Mom's cockroach casserole

Being the only one who thought
it was a costume party

Leaves falling
into my beak

Being late for
things

Feeling cold and wet

Here's my **FLAP-TASTIC** family.

Mom   Baby Mo   Dad

A Wingdale OWLoween

Me

Humphrey

This is Baxter, my **SWOOPER-DUPER** pet bat.

It's great being an owl!

We're covered in soft feathers.

We can turn our
heads almost all
the way around.

We can hear the tiniest noises with our **OWLMAZING** ears.

Oh! And we can fly!

I live in a tree house on Woodpine Avenue.

My best friend, Lucy Beakman, lives next door. (She's great at making puppets.)

My school – Treetop Owlementary –
is the best in the forest. Here's a photo
of my class.

Mrs. Featherbottom   Hailey
Jacob
Sue   Kiera
Zac   George
Carlos
                      Zara
Lilly   Me   Lucy
        Macy

Our homework was to dress up as a
farm animal on Monday. We don't know
<u>why</u> yet, but I'm guessing
there's going to be a
surprise! I'm dressing up as
a sheep. (They're so soft
and cuddly!) I can't wait to
see everyone's costumes!

♡ Counting Sheep ♡

Monday

I flew to school with Lucy.

Everyone's farm animal costumes were **OWLMAZING**!

Carlos: duck

Zac: goose

Macy: goat

Lilly: horse

Sue: cow

Jacob: pig

George: chicken

Lucy: sheepdog

Kiera: rooster

Hailey: donkey

Zara: llama

Why are you a cloud, Eva?

I'm a sheep.

Oh.

Mrs. Featherbottom, why are we dressed up like this?

Because . . . SURPRISE! We're going on a field trip to Poppy's Pumpkin Farm!

We all cheered. This was **SUPER FLAPPY** news, Diary!

Poppy's Pumpkin Farm is famous in our forest. And we always love hearing <u>The Story of the Thank-You Pumpkin</u> . . .

One autumn, a long time ago, everyone was hungry. It hadn't rained all summer and the land was very dry. There wasn't enough food.

The only food that grew was one huge, wild pumpkin. Instead of keeping it for themselves, the forest animals shared it with the farm animals.

From that day on, the farm has grown pumpkins. And every year — to say thank you — the farm makes food for all the forest animals' Falling Leaves Day parties.

The farm also grows and decorates one special MASSIVE pumpkin for everyone in the forest to see and enjoy. It's meant to remind us all that if we share, no one goes hungry.

That story always gets us excited about Falling Leaves Day.

I wonder how big the Thank-You Pumpkin will be this year!

The farm's pumpkin pie tastes SO good!

I love Falling Leaves Day!

Poppy's farm makes the food for all the Falling Leaves Day parties. So we're going to spend the next three days helping them. But first, we have a lot to learn about farm life!

We learned lots about farm animals:

Goats sneeze to warn others of danger!

Chickens have more bones in their necks than giraffes!

Cows can smell something up to six miles away!

Lucy, Hailey, and I flew home together.

I can't wait for our field trip!

I won't be able to sleep today!

Try counting sheep!

Counting sheep isn't working AT ALL, Diary! Instead it's made me even more excited about tomorrow! I'm going to be a <u>real</u> farmer for three days!

♡ Field Trip Time ♡

Tuesday

The first thing we saw when we flew to the farm was a field of big juicy pumpkins glowing in the moonlight!

First, Poppy showed us around.

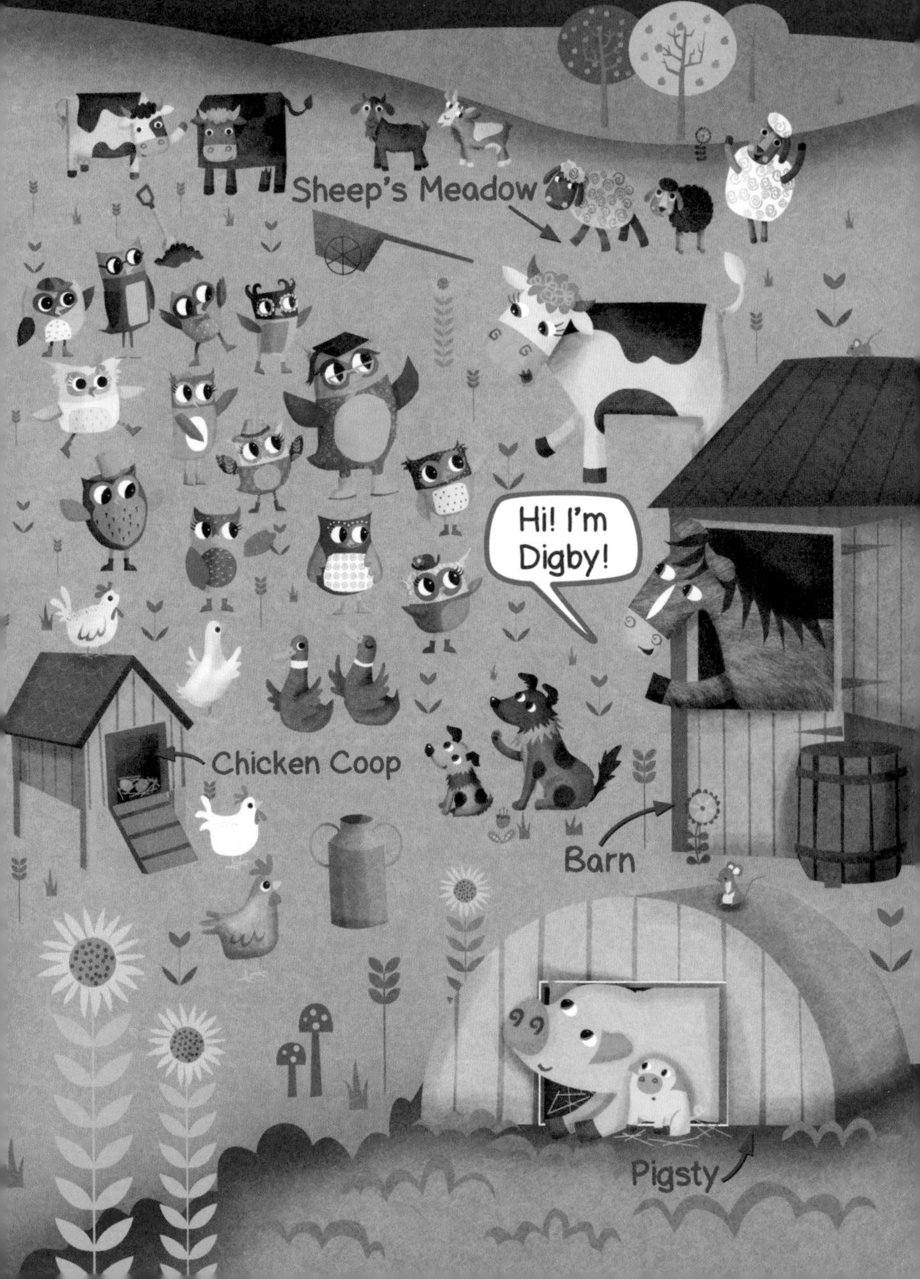

Then the animals taught us how to be good farmers.

The cows taught us how to get their milk.

The chickens taught us how to collect their eggs.

The horses taught us how to pick apples.

The sheepdogs taught us how to round up the sheep. (We round them up when it's time for the sheep chefs to bake the pumpkin pies.)

Now we're <u>really</u> ready to help on the farm tomorrow and Thursday!

At the end of the night, Digby pulled a cart across the farm. It held the biggest, brightest pumpkin I've ever seen: this year's Thank-You Pumpkin!

Thank you, Poppy, for always growing your Thank-You Pumpkin and for providing food for all the fall parties!

Thank you, owls, for coming to help us! See you tomorrow!

We learned a lot, Diary. Now, I'd better get to bed . . . Farmer Eva needs to be wide awake first thing tomorrow!

4

♥ Farm Detectives ♥

Wednesday

We were all **FLAPPING** and **HOOTING** on the way to the farm. We couldn't wait to do all the farm jobs we'd learned about yesterday.

But when we got there –

DISASTER!

The Thank-You Pumpkin was MISSING!

That wasn't even the worst thing, Diary! The worst thing was that – because of the lost pumpkin – the animals had been in a panic all day!

The cows were too nervous to make milk.

The chickens were too upset to lay eggs.

The horses were too sad to pick apples.

And the sheep chefs were so worried, they hadn't made any pies!

No farm work had been done <u>at all</u>!

Our pumpkin is gone! And now we've lost a full day of farm work! How will we ever be ready for the parties now??

The farm animals needed our help! We <u>needed</u> to solve the mystery of the missing pumpkin.

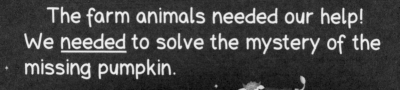

Poor Poppy! She and the whole farm worked so hard growing that special pumpkin.

We must find it!

Otherwise all the parties will be ruined!

We can't let that happen!

Let's start the
Farm Detectives Club!

Mrs. Featherbottom liked our club idea.
So she asked me, Hailey, Lucy, George,
and Zac to start detecting right away.

She asked everyone else to help the
farm animals get back to work.

The Farm Detectives Club's first job was to ask the farm animals if they'd seen anything strange before the pumpkin went missing.

Just then, a family of mice ran through the barn. Poppy shooed them away.

Those pesky mice! They never help out.

They're always getting under our hooves!

And they're always stealing our crumbs.

Suddenly, I had an idea.

Maybe the mice are hungry. Could they have taken the pumpkin?

Mice?! What would they want with a huge pumpkin?

Besides, they're too tiny to move something so big!

HA HA!

HA!

HA HA!

Everyone laughed, and I felt a bit silly.

We looked everywhere for the pumpkin. But we could not find it anywhere.

We saw how much work still had to get done on the farm! So we gave up our search for the night and helped out. (It was fun!)

At the end of the night, we flew home on tired wings.

Oh, Diary, how could such a GIANT pumpkin get so lost???

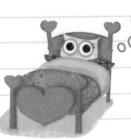

♥Find That Pumpkin!♥

Thursday

As soon as we got to the farm tonight, I called a club meeting.

I made these outfits for us — to help us be <u>real</u> detectives today.

I love this hat!

We flew after George as he told us his plan.

You can curl up into balls and roll out of the cart. Then we'll see where you roll to!

George pushed each of us out of the cart.

But we all rolled in different directions!

As I brushed off my feathers, the mice family scurried past.

We followed the mice
to a faraway hill.

And we found . . .

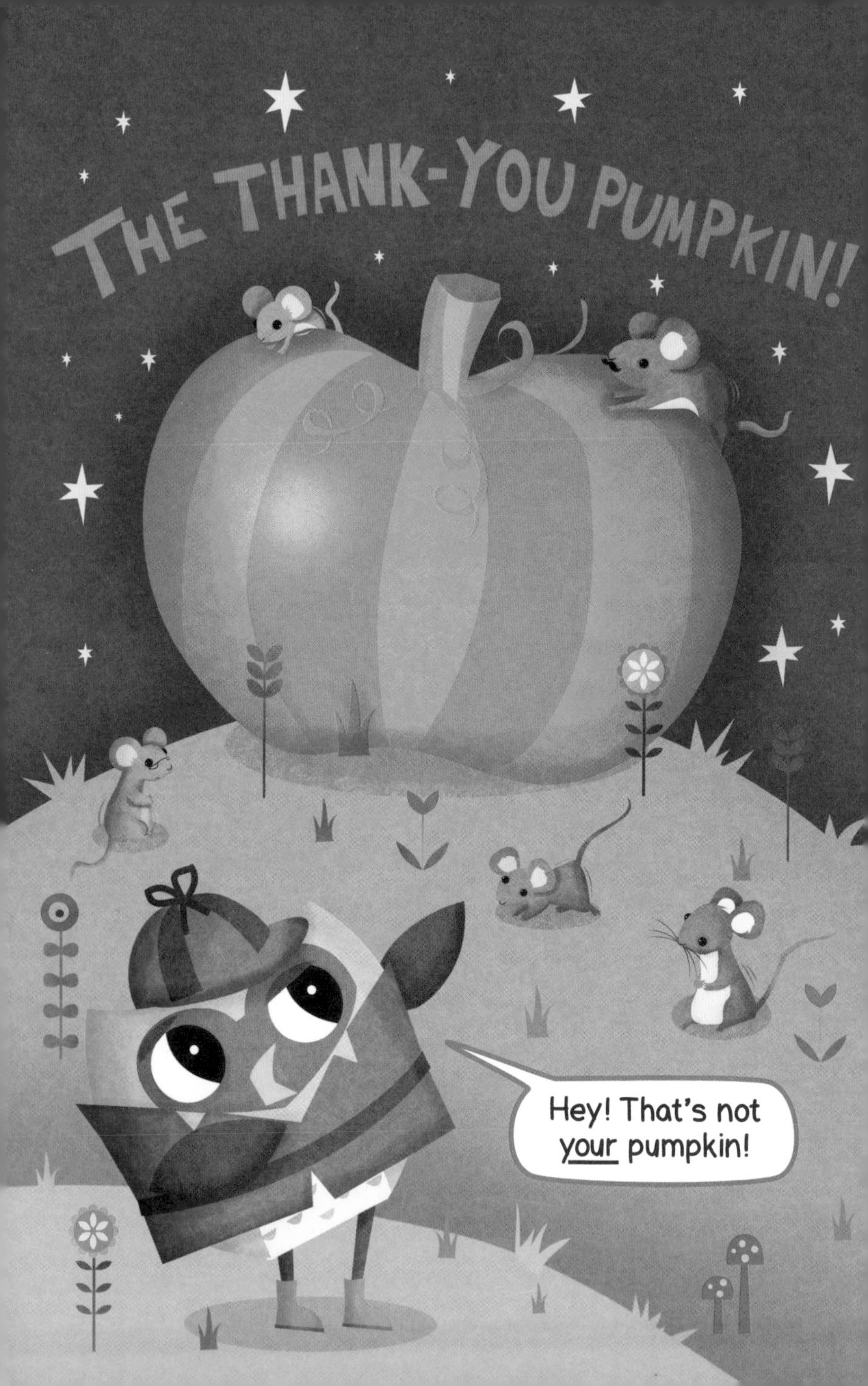
THE THANK-YOU PUMPKIN!
Hey! That's not your pumpkin!

George felt bad for yelling at the mice though because they didn't look like "thieves" at all. They looked sad, shivery, and hungry. They started talking in <u>really</u> quiet squeaks.

Hi. I'm Barry. Sorry. We just found this pumpkin, here on the hill.

So it <u>did</u> roll out of the cart!

We thought no one wanted it.

We tried to ask about it on the farm, but they never hear us.

We were hungry, and we wanted to make this our winter home.

But please take it back to the farm animals. And tell them we're sorry.

We rolled the pumpkin to the barn, but I felt bad about taking it from the mice.

When we told the farm animals it was the mice who took it, they were angry. But then we explained what <u>really</u> happened.

The thing is, they weren't trying to steal it.

The pumpkin had rolled out of the cart.

The mice found it.

They just wanted some food and a home.

They're sorry.

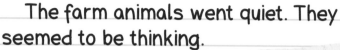

The farm animals went quiet. They seemed to be thinking.

We look after one another on the farm. We should have looked after the mice, too.

How can we make it up to them?

Well, you make such great stuff. Is there anything to spare?

Later that night, the farm animals took some presents to the mice.

And best of all, Poppy invited them to come live in the barn.

The mice were so happy! Barry wanted to thank Poppy, so I flew him up to her ear.

Thank you, Poppy!
We'd love to help out on the farm, too.
We're very good at making cheese!

That sounds great!

We were super busy all night — baking pies and other foods for the parties.

Then we rolled the Thank-You Pumpkin to the middle of the forest.

And we decorated it all together.

Do you have a big party on the farm, too?

No. We're much too tired after all this work to plan our own party.

But thank you again for all your help, NEIGH-bors!

Yes! Thank you! We couldn't have gotten it all done in time without you!

Oh, Diary, I just wish the farm animals had their own party to celebrate Falling Leaves Day. If only there was something I could do?!

♡ The First Falling Leaves ♡

Friday

The forest is wild with excitement!

We still have <u>lots</u> to do to get ready for Falling Leaves Day!

We wrote down everything we wanted to make for the party.

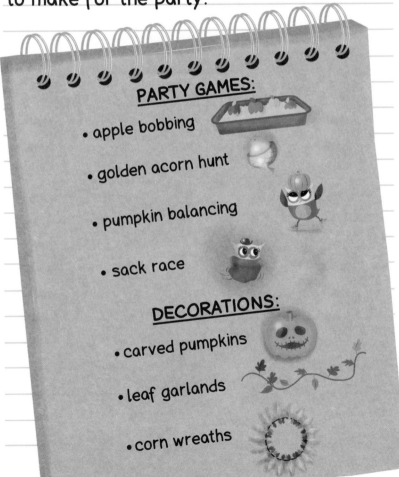

PARTY GAMES:

- apple bobbing

- golden acorn hunt

- pumpkin balancing

- sack race

DECORATIONS:

- carved pumpkins

- leaf garlands

- corn wreaths

We set to work making everything.

Then, Diary, I had a **FLAPPY-FABULOUS** idea!

At lunchtime, everyone liked my idea.

So we talked to Mrs. Featherbottom.

We'd like to invite the farm animals to <u>our</u> party!

What a thoughtful idea!

Next, we made a special invitation.
Do you like it, Diary?

YOU ARE INVITED TO

·THE OWLS'·
FALLING LEAVES PARTY!

WHEN: TOMORROW NIGHT
WHERE: THE OLD OAK TREE

Please come!

We flew to Poppy's Pumpkin Farm right away.

Surprise!

YOU ARE INVITED TO

·THE OWLS'·
FALLING LEAVES PARTY!

WHEN: TOMORROW NIGHT
WHERE: THE OLD OAK TREE
Please come!

After flying home, I ate Falling Leaves Day Eve dinner with my family. Mom made **BERRY-BUG SOUP** and toffee apples!

Then Lucy called me on my **PINEPHONE**.

Look outside, Eva!

Wow! The first leaves are falling!

Tomorrow is going to be the BEST Falling Leaves Day EVER! How am I ever going to sleep?!

♡ Pumpkin Pie for All! ♡

Saturday

HOOT HOOT!

Happy Falling Leaves Day! Lucy and Hailey came over to my tree house to get ready. We made leaf jewelry to wear to the party.

What do you think, Diary?

We met Mrs. Featherbottom and the rest of our class at the Old Oak Tree to help set up.

The Thank-You Pumpkin looked so **OWLSOME**. The leaves were falling and everything looked **HOOTIFUL**!

Soon, the party was in full swing!

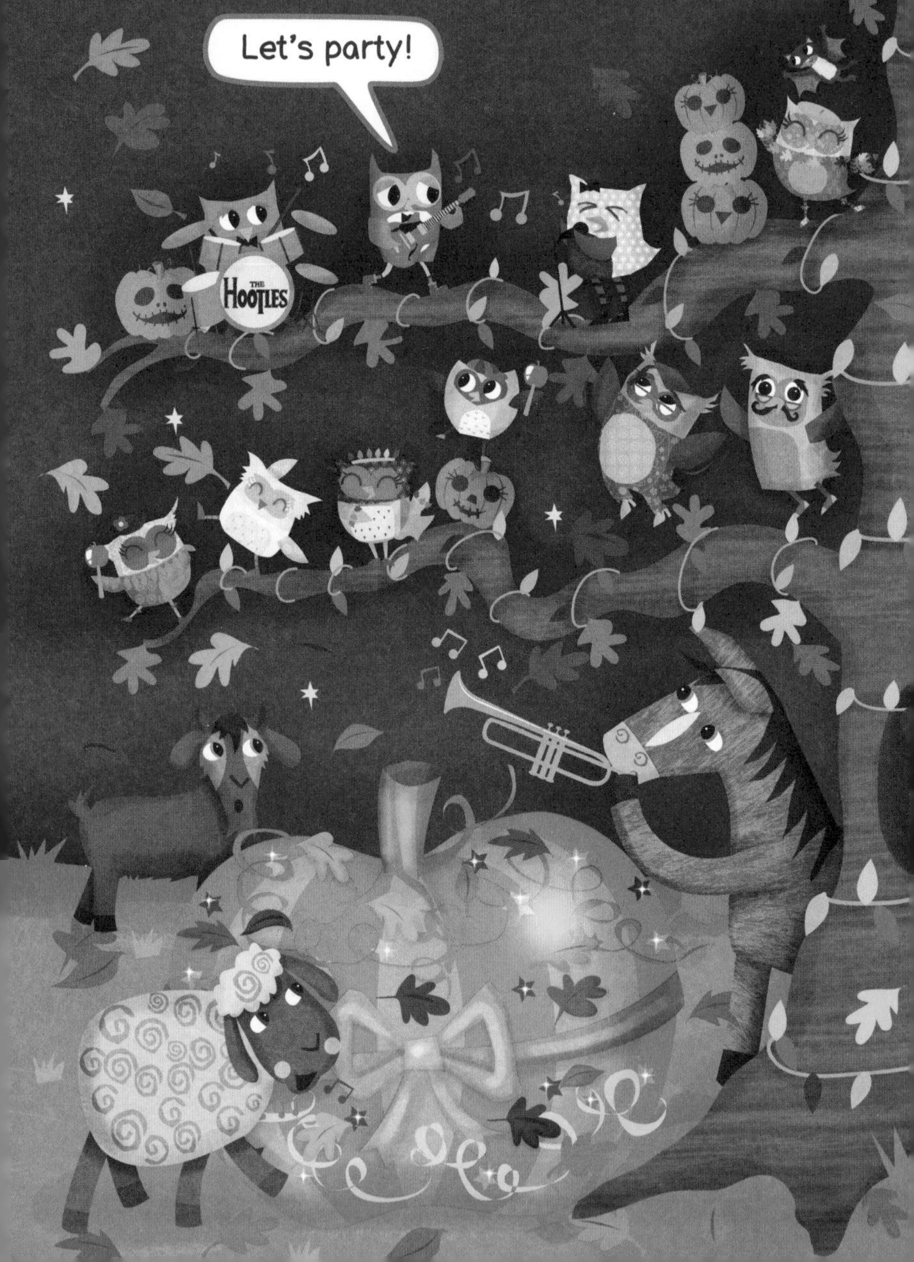

We ate oodles of pumpkin pie and mouse cheese. It was all SO yummy scrummy!

The horses won the apple bobbing game.

The goats won the pumpkin-balancing contest.

The mice won the golden acorn hunt.

And we won the sack race!

Then Mr. Swoopstone, the mayor of Treetopolis, flew up to the microphone.

Thank you to the farm animals for partying with us and for their delicious food.

Thank you for inviting us. And thank you to the owlets who helped us at the farm and to the owl detectives who found the Thank-You Pumpkin. You have all reminded us of what this special time of year is really about — giving, sharing, and being thankful.

Happy Falling Leaves Day, everyone!

Toward the end of the party, I heard a small squeak. The mice wanted to say something.

Shhh!

Everyone, listen!

Thank you for letting me squeak. We are so thankful for your food and kindness. But there are lots more animals with small voices in the forest who are hungry. Maybe we could give our leftovers to them?

It was a **FLAP-TASTIC** idea! So we piled up the leftover food and took it to any animals who needed it.

Sharing our food with others was the best part of the night. Well, that and when my family and I ate our last delicious slices of pumpkin pie.

I have so much to be thankful for — wonderful food, friends, family, and a warm tree house. What more does a small owl need?

See you next time, Diary.

Rebecca Elliott was a lot like Eva when she was younger: She loved making things and hanging out with her best friends. Now that Rebecca is older, not much has changed — except that her best friends are her husband, Matthew, and their children. She still loves making things, like stories, cakes, music, and paintings. But as much as she and Eva have in common, Rebecca cannot fly or turn her head all the way around. No matter how hard she tries.

Rebecca is the author of JUST BECAUSE and MR. SUPER POOPY PANTS. OWL DIARIES is her first early chapter book series.

OWL DIARIES

How much do you know about Trip to the Pumpkin Farm?

Why is the Thank-You Pumpkin special? Reread pages 16–17.

Farmers have many important jobs on a farm. In this story, what are four of their jobs? Reread pages 24–25.

The Farm Detectives Club finds the missing pumpkin. Who has it? How do <u>you</u> think Eva feels when she learns what they wanted to use the pumpkin for?

Two of Eva's favorite things to do in the autumn are playing in leaf piles and getting cozy. What are two of your favorite autumn activities?

The farm animals work together to help take care of the mice. How can you help out in <u>your</u> community? Use words and pictures to describe what you can do.